THE PROM